for Nadia

First published in Great Britain in August 2015 by Bloomsbury Publishing Plc
Published in the United States of America in May 2016 by Bloomsbury Children's Books
www.bloomsbury.com

Bloomsbury is a registered trademark of Bloomsbury Publishing Plc

For information about permission to reproduce selections from this book, write to
Permissions, Bloomsbury Children's Books, 1385 Broadway, New York, New York 10018
Bloomsbury books may be purchased for business or promotional use. For information on bulk purchases please contact
Macmillan Corporate and Premium Sales Department at specialmarkets@macmillan.com

Library of Congress Cataloging-in-Publication Data
available upon request
ISBN 978-1-61963-975-1 (hardcover)
ISBN 978-1-61963-976-8 (e-book) • ISBN 978-1-61963-977-5 (e-PDF)

Art created with watercolors • Typeset in Cambria • Book design by Goldy Broad
Printed in China by Leo Paper Products, Heshan, Guangdong
2 4 6 8 10 9 7 5 3 1

All papers used by Bloomsbury Publishing, Inc., are natural, recyclable products made from wood grown in well-managed forests.
The manufacturing processes conform to the environmental regulations of the country of origin.

I'm a Girl!

Yasmeen Ismail

BLOOMSBURY
NEW YORK LONDON OXFORD NEW DELHI SYDNEY

I'm **supposed** to be *nice* . . .

all **sugar** and **spice** . . .

but I'm **sweet** *and* **sour,**
not a little flower!

Just watch me go—
always *fast*, never slow.

I'm a girl . . .

I'm a girl!

And I am as **brave** as anyone else I know.

I like to be **spontaneous**
and do things my **own** way.
When I do, it's **much more FUN!**

I'm a girl!

I'm a girl . . .

I want to learn **everything**—I'd like to know **a lot.**
My brain is **FULL** of "knowing things."

I like to play games—**all sorts** of games.
There's no **right** or **wrong** way to
play when you play **"pretend."**

It's okay to want to be
good at things.

I like to be the BEST.

I'm a girl!

I'm a ...

boy!

Being us is SUPER!